GHANA

YANKEY

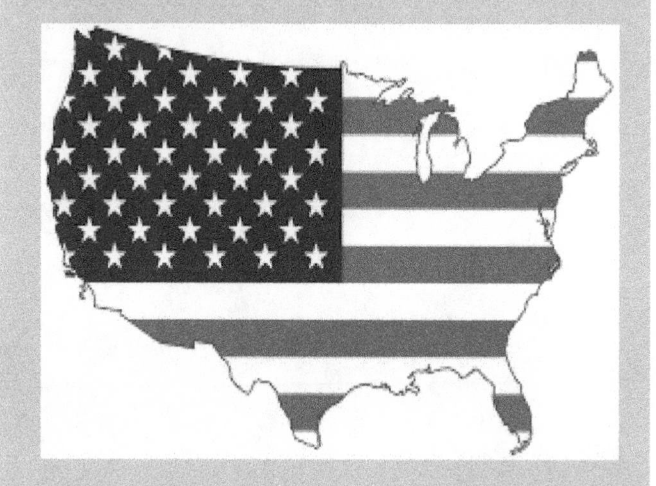

I AM MY RELATIVE'S ASPIRATIONS

From the shores of Ghana to the
streets of Yankey

I hold on to my dreams

Even though the hassle goes on

I don't give up

-Sasha Yaa Badu

THE SHIMMIGRANT

Marjy Marj

Dear Susan,
Happy Reading!
Marjy Marj

Dear Susan,

Happy Reading!

Marie Ma

Triple A Press

A3

To Bill and Sally-

The parents who sacrificed for me to live my dream

To Kofi and Adom-

The wind beneath my wings

Acknowledgements – Forever Grateful

I stand on the shoulders of my network. Without you, there is no story.

I learn from the experiences of those that have come before me. Without you, we have no history.

I am inspired by the newer generations. Because of you, we can prepare for the future.

To my sweet Hajia Meimuna who shared stories of Ash Town when we were younger – I will never forget your kindness.

To my mama Sally, who experienced living in a polygamous environment – I adore you.

To my friends who worked as house helps growing up – Thank you for your sacrifice.

To my sisters and brothers who immigrated to the great Yankey and Babylon – The dream lives on.

To Boss Kofi and Adomski - You make my world work.

Note

This is a story of fiction.

The real Ashanti New Town (Ash Town)

is not a village.

It is a suburb of Kumasi.

See back pages for:

List of Characters

Timeline

Glossary

im.mi.grant:

a person who comes to a country to take up permanent residence

-Merriam Webster Dictionary

shi.mmi.grant:

a female who lives permanently in a foreign country she calls home

-The Shimmigrant

A SAFE PLACE

Oh such sweet memories.
The days when we woke up to the cock
crowing at dawn.
We danced like there was no tomorrow.
We roamed the streets of Ash Town like
'Don Dadas' and 'King Kongs'.
We owned the days and the nights!
If only I could turn back the clock.

Back to those carefree days!

Walayi!

CURRENT SITUATION

PART I – The Early Days

PART II – The In Between

PART III - Today

CURRENT SITUATION

YANKEY OHH YANKEY!

This Yankey life is full of ups and downs. Curveball after curveball. I thought living in Yankey would be the answer to all my problems.

'Chai', was I wrong.

This America! Everyday so so 'wahala'. Paycheck come, paycheck go.

This Yankey life is not what I imagined oo! The hustle here is real papa! Since I came to America, I have worked so hard! Meanwhile I can't even catch a break.

Every night, I go to bed praying for my breakthrough.

A part of me dreads the future. Will I always be financially strapped?

When I see the bills and my mounting debt, I wonder if I made the right decision to stay in Yankey.

Sometimes the success stories about the folks back home make me feel like a loser. There are days when I wonder if I'll be better off relocating to Kumasi.

But then I can't see myself going back empty handed. After all these years? No. That will be shameful.

So, I must stay and make the best of this Yankey life. Maybe one day it'll get better. My breakthrough may be coming.

I envision living in the suburbs with my three kids. A two-car garage won't be bad. Maybe I will be a proper American and have a dog too. A Golden Retriever will be perfect.

Chai! The conditions will be removed. I will get that paper.

That elusive American dream is on its way.

I must believe!

My God reigns!

PART I

THE EARLY DAYS

BIRTH OF A WARRIOR

BIRTH OF A WARRIOR

So I'm going to tell you about the story of my birth as told by my Mama.

I am Sasha Badu. My traditional name is Obaa Yaa Piesie. Obaa stands for girl. Yaa basically means a female born on Thursday. Piesie means I am the first born child of my parents.

I was born at home on a hot evening. I like to think that there was a lot of pomp and pageantry surrounding my entrance into this world but truth be told, it was a simple birth.

When my mom went into labor, my dad and grandmothers panicked. Mama was about 35 weeks pregnant and was not expecting her first child to be born that early.

That Thursday started like any other day. The house was bustling with activity when Mama woke up. As a newly married woman, she had moved in with her husband's family. The compound house was home to my paternal grandparents, several uncles, aunties and cousins.

Like my dad's sisters, Mama was a trader. On the morning of my birth, my grandmother prepared a bowl of porridge and some tea bread for breakfast. VIP treatment for the woman carrying her son's child.

The meal was even more delicious because Mama spread some blue band margarine on the bread.

As she sat under the mango tree enjoying her breakfast, Mama couldn't help but to fantasize about the future. The elders had assured her that based on how she was carrying the pregnancy, it was likely that she would have a girl.

In her mind, she could see her daughter winning awards at school. She imagined herself sitting at a Speech and Prize Giving day - hearing her daughter's name over and over again.

Enough of the daydreaming. Mama couldn't fantasize forever, she had to pick up her basin and get to work.

She was a street vendor. Her basin was filled with washing soap, cooking oil and a few other grocery items.

As Mama patrolled the streets with her items, she felt this strange pain going through her back. Being a cautious pregnant woman, she thought it was probably due to the heavy load that she was carrying on her head. For the sake of her pregnancy, she made a mental note to lessen her load next time.

Mama walked for about 4 miles across different neighborhoods advertising her products. She shouted on top of her lungs: "aduane o, tin tomantoes, cooking oils, key soap…fofoofo."

The fofoofo was the key. Mama's items were cheaper than the average seller's.

She almost sold all the items in her basin! However, since her pain was getting worse, she hopped on the homebound 'trotro' bus.

Within a few minutes, after arriving home, she felt something trickle down her legs. Little did she know that it was her water that had broken. The abdominal cramp-like pain was excruciating. Mama was screaming on top of her lungs.

My grandmother sprang into action. She laid a mat for Mama and hurriedly sent for the local midwife. She also sent word to Maa, my maternal grandmother. Within 30 minutes, Maa and the midwife had arrived.

Both grandmas sat by Mama as Auntie Vivian, the midwife wiped her forehead. They fanned her, gave her water to drink and assured her she will be okay.

According to Mama, things progressed really fast after Auntie Vivian and Maa's arrival.

With encouragement from the women, Mama began to push. The delivery process was underway. Within a matter of minutes, a tiny baby girl was born.

Mama was thrilled, yet scared for her pale baby girl.

Because I was born a few weeks early, my family was worried about my survival. In addition to looking pale, my eyes had a yellowish tint.

The midwife advised them to put me on a pile of broomsticks, swathe me in a cloth, and put lanterns around me.

Mama said, although I was a tiny baby, she could tell that I was a fighter. I responded well to treatment. Within three days, I looked like a healthy and radiant baby girl.

Seven days after my birth, my family held a traditional naming ceremony in my honor.

They invited the elders, extended family and friends to the ceremony. My paternal grandmother held me as my grandfather put a taste of water and alcohol on my tongue. The symbolic act was to teach me the importance of telling the truth at all times.

I received my traditional name that day
- Yaa Asantewaa Badu aka Obaa Yaa.

I was named after the great warrior - Yaa Asantewaa, queen mother of Ejisu in the Ashanti empire.

A few weeks later, my parents added an English name – Sasha. They named me after the richest woman in Ash Town.

Fondly called Maame 'Broni', Auntie Sasha was married to Dr. Osei, the most popular doctor in Ash Town. 'Doctor' was famous because he trained in Russia. Everybody wanted to go to the 'aburokyire' doctor (foreign-trained doctor) when they were sick. It was always an added bonus to catch a glimpse of his 'white' wife. Auntie Sasha was the richest woman in Ash Town. Maybe Dada wanted me to become as rich as Auntie Sasha some day!

Sasha Obaa Yaa Asantewaa Badu, daughter of Kwame and Ama of Kumasi was ready for the world!

MEMORIES

MEMORIES

I have a vivid recollection of a fight between my grandmothers because Mama had failed to give my father a second child. A few weeks after that fight, my first stepmother arrived at the family house. Everybody celebrated. Even Mama seemed to be part of that celebration.

In the western world, the arrival of my second mother would have been considered polygamous. However, this practice was acceptable in our culture.

To date, I am amazed at the enthusiasm with which my mother welcomed my dad's other wives into our lives. Mama received dad's second wife with such grace and dignity.

Before long, I had another sibling, and then another and on and on…

When I was about six years old, we moved from my paternal grandmother's house to our own compound house.

With the new house came a new stepmother. I don't know why, but Dada felt the need to marry a third wife. Our family was growing. I had several siblings to play and fight with. Our home was always bustling with activity.

Some of our best memories were made sitting under the mango tree. We shared Kwaku Ananse stories and played games. Those nights were filled with laughter. I loved to dance under the tree. Oh, how I enjoyed entertaining my siblings!

My trademark dance moves earned me a nickname. The siblings called me 'nankonhwea' because of my skinny legs.

I miss those days oo. If only I could go back to being a carefree kid.

GOOD BLACK MEDICINE

GOOD BLACK MEDICINE

Over the years, my Mama's personality changed. The inability to bear additional children for my dad had taken a toll on her. She was no longer the happy go lucky person from the earlier years.

As a result of her desperate need to have more children, Mama resorted to visiting different pastors and herbalists.

Our go to herbalist was Papa Gyan. Once a month, we will visit Papa in his hut. He lived in a village on the outskirts of Kumasi. We traveled by boneshaker and then by foot.

Papa was a holy and revered man. We always took off our shoes and covered our heads before entering his hut.

During our visits, Papa poured libation and called on the ancestors. He started by calling 'Twedeampon Nyame' the omnipotent god, then he called on 'Asaase Yaa' - mother earth.

As a sign of appreciation, we always offered Papa gifts. We will place the items by the shrine and watch him perform customary rites.

Papa was known to be a soothsayer. He had the ability to predict the future. There was even a rumor that Papa had predicted that Ghana will be ruled by Johns until the presidency of the man with a royal name. Maybe Papa had a special gift!

Despite his inexpensive fees, several important people traveled from afar to seek healing and guidance from Papa Gyan.

I always sat in awe when we visited him. I was amazed by his popularity. In my eyes, Papa was a magician. He had healed so many, including my bedridden uncle!

Mama always adhered to Papa's instruction. After every consultation, he will pray for her, give her herbs, and offer a substance to sprinkle around the bedroom. He also gave me 'boto' for my health.

'Boto' was the powdery substance that I licked every morning when I was growing up. Mama said it was good for my health.

HOLY GHOST FIRE

HOLY GHOST FIRE

Our healing journey did not end with Papa Gyan. Mama and I were regulars at church revivals too.

Although I didn't trust some of those miracle working pastors. Mama, was a different story. She believed in the new breed of charismatic pastors in Kumasi.

Any given Friday evening, you will find us at a different Revival. We visited the popular 'powerful' pastors. Those church members prayed in tongues. Hopping from one church to the other, was our norm.

There were times when I feared going to the charismatic churches. Too much jumping and screaming!

I was scared that I may end up being possessed by some evil spirit. The revivals and all night services were pretty intensive. People prayed very loudly and fell on the floor easily.

Every time people started falling, I will hold on to Mama for dear life.

Although I was scared, Mama insisted that it was important for us to go to church together. She did not want any evil to befall me.

I remember this episode from one of the demon casting revivals:

A beautiful young lady approached the priest during the altar call portion of the service. She had repented of her sins and wanted to give her life to Christ.

As she walked forward, the pastor started screaming that evil spirits were approaching the presence of the anointed. He called on elders to come forward. Then they started praying for this woman.

To my surprise, the woman started speaking in different voices. I mean, she spoke in the voice of a man, a child, a girl!! She was speaking different dialects. It was so scary! I was terrified!!

The pastor and his people said she was possessed by demons and that she was married in the spirit. The pastor even said that she had spiritual kids and would have difficulty conceiving in real life.

Look, I kid you not. I wanted to run out of the church.

Mama held my hand tightly and told me not to open my eyes. She said that by praying harder, I would prevent any evil from entering my body.

Can you imagine? As young as I was? I was petrified and was on the verge of peeing in my pants.

After the service, the young lady was escorted to the back offices for additional prayers.

We never visited that church again!

But we didn't stop visiting different churches. We probably visited a total of 12 churches, searching for Mama's miracle.

Now that I'm older, I can confidently say that some of those pastors are guilty of abuse.

I witnessed an outright beating during one of the services at Bantama. There was this nicely dressed woman who needed prayers because she wanted to have a child.

When the priest asked people to come forward for prayers, the lady joined the group at the altar.

Lo and behold, the priest pushed her down and started stomping on her. As the woman screamed, the priest said the barrenness within her was finally leaving. He promised that the lady would come back with a baby in 9 months.

You should have seen how the woman danced and jubilated after the stomping and beating.

Surprisingly, nobody seemed to think that the pastor was wrong. The woman was very happy that she had been delivered of her barrenness.

Maybe she ended up having 10 or 0 children. Who knows?

The drama at the charismatic churches did not stop us from visiting. Mama was convinced that the prayers were going to help her conceive.

WHEN IT IS COMING

WHEN IT IS COMING

Every third Saturday we made a trip to Papa's hut. This particular visit felt different. Although Mama had been feeling unwell for about two weeks, she did not want to miss her routine trip. Despite her nausea, we boarded the boneshaker to Papa's.

The journey felt longer than usual. I kept stealing glances at Mama. I was wondering what could be wrong with her.

As a 9-year-old girl, I was scared that my mother had contracted malaria. However, I was optimistic that everything will be resolved by Papa.

The walk from the station to Papa's hut felt longer that day. We had to make a few stops because Mama was dizzy. Finally, we arrived at the hut.

However, there was a ton of people waiting in line. Unfortunately, the wait was too much for Mama. She passed out.

I thought she had died. I kept calling her but she wouldn't respond. My world was spinning. What was wrong with my Mama. My screams didn't go unnoticed. Some of Papa's visitors rushed to our aid.

They revived Mama by pouring water over her body. My heart was throbbing. I didn't know what to do. I didn't even remember to pray.

Thankfully, we were able to skip the rest of the line because of Mama's condition.

Upon entering the hut, I was relieved to hear Papa's calm voice. He touched Mama's face, mixed some herbs for her and called on the ancestors to intervene.

Papa gazed at Mama for maybe 2 minutes. You could hear a pin drop in the room. Then came the news.

Papa told Mama that she was with child. She was carrying twins!

Mama was beside herself. She bowed to Papa and thanked him for the reassuring prognosis. We believed in miracles!

Papa mixed some herbs for Mama's nourishment. I guess the herbs were probably her prenatal meds.

On our ride back, I wondered about the meaning of religion. How was it possible for Papa to perform miracles, heal the sick and speak to the ancestors?

If Papa's West African Traditional religion could heal the sick and do good, why did the Christian pastors condemn Papa's religious practice?

I never saw Papa beat or stomp on anyone. He was always gentle and spoke in a reassuring voice. His medicine was good for us when we were sick.

When I shared my thoughts with Mama, she provided a simple answer. Both pastors and traditional priests prayed to God. She didn't find anything wrong with either method.

Despite my misgivings about religion and faith, we were delighted about Mama's pregnancy. As we stepped off the boneshaker, she looked at me, smiled, and said - "When it is coming, it is doing."

WONDERFUL WONDERS

WONDERFUL WONDERS

As the months went by, Mama's belly grew bigger. Papa was right. 2 human beings lived in her belly. I was very excited. Finally, my Mama's wishes were coming to pass. Everybody in our household was happy for her. I never saw or heard any resentment from my other mothers.

The twins arrived when I was 10 years old. We named them Panyin (older twin) and Kakra (younger twin).

Mama attributed her pregnancy to the interventional methods employed by her herbalists and pastors. No one could convince her otherwise.

All of my stepmothers were excited for Mama. As the senior wife, she had treated them fairly and welcomed them into the fold.

The twins' outdooring ceremony was a big fiesta. We had the naming ceremony on a Saturday morning. The whole neighborhood must have come to our house that day. There was a lot to eat and drink! Everybody wore white.

Although I had to run a lot of errands, I did not mind. It was a wonderful celebration.

The singing and dancing was phenomenal!

No be easy kind of celebrations. Plenty chow for everyone!

Hmm, now that I live abroad, I wonder how my family pulled off our celebrations.

I mean, Dada was a driver's mate with four wives. That alone was a miracle!

Mama was a street vendor who had progressed from selling everyday groceries to 'obroni wawu' (second hand) clothing.

Two of my stepmothers worked as aides at a chop bar (restaurant).

My other stepmother sold bofrot (doughnuts) by the roadside.

How in the world did we afford all those celebrations?

Somehow the Badus of Ashanti New Town made it work. We were the beneficiaries of communal living. Our extended family had each other's back.

Chai! Our family was alright!

LIVING BADU

LIVING BADU

We didn't have a lot of money growing up so our options were limited. We slept on the floor, used makeshift bathrooms, attended government schools, wore second hand clothing, ate leftovers and pretty much took care of ourselves because our parents had to work all day.

Our lifestyle was quite basic. We didn't even have the luxury of using commodes. When we had to go, our only option was to use a pit latrine behind the house. My cousin fondly named the pit '*who dey for top*'. The nickname was derived from the flies that circled our 'butts' while we squatted to ease ourselves.

If we needed to go at night, we used a kerosene lantern as a guide. I used to be so scared to walk out at night because of stories of the witches who patrolled the night. My poor siblings. I was always waking somebody up because I was too scared to walk by myself.

Can you imagine waking up in the middle of the night and needing to go right away? Well, in my case, you didn't have a choice but to hold it.

There were times that it was no joke running to the pit latrine. You were not even worried about going on yourself. You just didn't want your poop to trickle down inside the house!

Although our options were limited, our predicament was our normal. We did not know any different.

We did as we were told, ate what we were given and basically did not have the right to complain about anything. That was just how life was. You did not smart mouth your parents because you wanted new shoes. You did not get to watch different channels on television. Heck, you made up our own TV shows!

The weekends were the best time for creativity. We even had singing groups with makeshift microphones. We used buckets and cans for musical instruments. We found interesting ways to entertain ourselves.

The weekdays, on the other hand, were more regimented because of school.

Our morning started with dawn prayers in the courtyard. It was mandatory for us to assemble under the mango tree every morning. Dada was the only one who did not show up at the prayers. After all, he was the head of our household and could do as he pleased.

The prayers were a chore. None of the kids wanted to wake up that early.

The worst part was the mothers' long intense prayers. The exhortations about the mighty and wonderful works of God seemed never ending. Sometimes, I will lie prostrate on the floor like I was in the spirit and go to sleep.

After prayers, we scrambled to finish our morning chores. We staggered our bathing times because of the limited bathing space. While the adults used the one indoor bathroom, the rest of us had to take turns bathing in the makeshift 'bathrooms' in the yard.

Our makeshift bathrooms comprised of cement blocks. The stacked up blocks provided us with a little privacy. The boys used one space and the girls used the other.

Each morning, I will find a bucket, fill it with a few pails of water and head to the bathroom. Sometimes I had to share the space with my sisters. We had fun giggling and dancing when we took those communal baths. We didn't want to be late for school so we raced each other.

Breakfast comprised of bread and some type of porridge. Sometimes I was lucky to receive a teaspoon of milk to sweeten my breakfast.

We walked to school every morning. The morning walks to school were brisk and fun. You could hear us approaching from a distance because of our local chorus tunes. There were times when we pretended to be part of a musical group. We called ourselves, The 'Anigye' Singers. Anigye meant happy in our local language.

Sometimes there were a few fights here and there. However, most of our morning walks were uneventful.

The walk back home was full of chatter. This was our time to reminisce about the day.

Despite having to do chores at home after school, we still managed to study before dinner. Luckily for us, one of our cousins was a class 2 teacher. His name was Bro. Kwabena. He tutored us 3 times a week - Mondays, Wednesdays and Fridays.

Bro. Kwabena, showed up at every session with his cane. His teaching style was a one size fit all approach. Although we were in different grades, he taught all of us.

Thanks to Bro. Kwabena, I mastered the times table. Considering that most of our family members performed menial jobs, we thought we were lucky to be related to a teacher.

Bro. Kwabena had nice clothes and a motorbike. We were motivated to go to school because we knew that if we studied hard, we will have nice clothes like him or marry someone who had a motorbike.

You should have seen the girls who used to ride with Bro. Kwabena, He was very popular in our neighborhood. Most ladies wanted to talk to him.

Thanks to Bro. Kwabena, my brothers were serious about their studies. Their dream was to work hard, purchase motorbikes and give girls rides.

Funny right? I guess the aspiration to give motorbike rides motivated them to study hard. The career expectations were not high for us 'saito' kids. Saito was the name used for kids in the public school system.

Our education standards were lower than the private schools. Most of the time, the kids in my neighborhood grew up to do menial jobs around town whilst the private school kids went on to the best secondary schools and colleges. The private school kids were destined to have the better jobs.

Thanks to Bro. Kwabena, there were a few of the saito kids who went on to do great things! One of the older saito kids from back in the day works at the Ghana Commercial Bank. Another one owns a printing press in Kumasi.

For people like us, having a white collar job was an anomaly. Very few people from my neighborhood made it out of the polygamous compound-house environment.

We just didn't have access to the rich people's schools and resources. We didn't have private tutors or brand new clothes.

No. We were lucky if we had electricity or water in our homes.

We did chores and worked for our upkeep. We even worked to pay off our family's debt.

I'm not saying that we were happy to do the work. No. there were several instances that I dragged my feet at chores. But I didn't have a choice. I had to sell 'ice water' to help my family make ends meet.

Back in the day, my siblings and I were trusted ice water sellers.

Although most people did not have refrigerators, they enjoyed drinking cold water. The Badu children sold the best ice water in town.

Mama purchased the ice blocks from the Presbyterian church.

Every day after school, I will prepare my ice water bucket and hit the streets.

I walked around screaming "ice water, cool your heart." Always came back home with an empty bucket.

After a hard day's work, the Badus congregated for dinner. The best part of the meals was reserved for the adults.

The kids ate together. Communal eating was the best! I learned a lot of life skills from my siblings during mealtime.
Dinner was what we called 'survival of the fittest!' We practiced chop time, no friend.

About four of us ate from the same bowl. You had to eat fast if you wanted a fair portion. My brothers were fast eaters so I had to adopt a strategy to keep up with them.

I'm sure if they moved to America, it'd be easy for them to win eating contests.

After dinner, we cleaned dishes and swept the compound. It was fun hanging around to hear the latest 'nsekuo' (gossip). Sometimes we overheard the mothers discussing the other neighbors and their problems.

Neighborhood news was never in short supply.

After the chores, we all gravitated towards our favorite spot. Under the mango tree!
This is when the 'tolee' was in abundance. We cracked jokes and laughed at each other.

With our limited resources, we found our happy place. We felt on top of the world. It's like we were the 'don dadas' of our world.

FIRST CRUSH

FIRST CRUSH

Jahel was this cute boy who lived in our neighborhood. He was the smartest boy at our school. Unlike us, Jahel and his family lived in a self-contained house. His parents owned a 'store'. If you wanted to buy minerals (soda) or the best biscuits, you could find it at Jahel's parents' store.

When we were kids, we used to play a neighborhood best friend game. We made a circle and took turns singing about our friends. At the end of every song, we will call our 'super' friend to the middle of the circle for a dance. There were so many a times that I wanted to call Jahel to the middle, but I never had the guts.

See, I had the biggest crush on him and really wanted him to notice me. All my siblings knew about my crush and used to tease me about it. But it seemed that Jahel was oblivious to my affection.

I couldn't wait to see him in the mornings though.

Every morning, I will put shea butter on my lips before our walk to school. My heart will start fluttering whenever we got close to Jahel's house.

I could predict his morning moves. He would walk out of their shop in his starched clothes. He always had a nice pair of shoes. Oh, and he carried a nice backpack too. It looked like he was stepping out of a TV show.

Although I walked with the girls in our group, I glanced at the boys often. I was fond of leading the local chorus. I thought that maybe if my voice stood out, Jahel was going to notice me.

Talk about stalking. I joined the Agric club because of him. Every other afternoon, the members of the club worked at the school farm. Never mind that I didn't like to weed at home. I cherished the hours that the club spent on the farm.

It didn't matter that Jahel barely acknowledged me.

Even after I moved away from home, I fantasized about him. I used to imagine how being married to him will feel like.

I envisioned us living in a self-contained house with a gate. We were probably going to live in Santaase or Nhyiaeso.

Back then, I was convinced that Jahel and I were destined to be together one day.

DESPERATE TIMES

DESPERATE TIMES

The year was 1983 and my family was in for a surprise. '83 was a hard year. As a result of dry spells and bushfires, Ghana was hit hard with famine. For some reason several migrants arrived in the country as well. Times were hard. It seemed like the money was vanishing from most households. People started watching their purchases more closely. The hard times took a toll on us.

With food prices at an all-time high, people were not interested in buying Mama's second hand clothes. Unfortunately for her, that meant that she couldn't pay her creditors. As the days went by, she found herself sinking further into debt.

Before long, the government announced a sharp increase in fuel costs. With gas prices skyrocketing, transportation costs went up too. The increase in 'trotro' fees didn't bode too well for families.

People opted to walk to the shorter destinations. Since Dada was a driver's mate, the demand for his services dwindled. As a result, he lost his job.

Can you imagine the predicament in our household?

Dada had always been an honest hardworking man. Losing his job took a toll on him. Here he was, jobless with four wives and seventeen kids. Yeah, you heard me. That was our situation!

Talk about a bruised ego. Dada became melancholy. He stopped playing 'ludu' and 'oware' (games) with us. I hardly saw him talking to the adults in the house.

With limited resources, Dada was a broken man. Most days, you will find him sitting under the neighborhood orange tree. His head bowed. Never uttering a word. The man had lost confidence in himself.

Thankfully, my siblings and I did not have to pay tuition at our government school. So even though we were broke, we could still attend school. Our school uniforms may have been tattered and our shoes worn out, but our spirits were resilient.

Luckily for our family, we didn't have to go to bed hungry during the famine days. Thanks to my two stepmothers who worked at the chop bar (restaurant), we enjoyed the customers' leftovers at dinnertime. However, there were those days in between where we had to fast during the day and eat bread for dinner.

The holidays were tough. I remember boiling stones in a pot for several hours. We called it pretend soup. We will always take the pot of stones inside the room and pretend we were having a feast. It was our normal. We thought other people did that too.

As I got older, I began to appreciate the reason why we boiled stones. Mama did not want our neighbors to know that we did not have the means to cook the sumptuous holiday meals.

Although we survived the harsh 1983 days, our family dynamic had changed by the end of the year.

Our parents thought long and hard about giving us a better life. Thus, they began contemplating about placing some of their children in servitude. They couldn't afford to watch our family suffer.

MATTER
DON COME

MATTER DON COME

February 4, 1984 was a special day. Mama made 'oto' for all of us in the morning because it was my twelfth birthday. I was a happy camper.

That morning, I wore my flowing red dress from the "Bend down Boutique." The plan was to visit Jahel's store. I was all smiles. I looked cute. Jahel was definitely going to notice me. I said to myself 'today be today, matter don come.' I was feeling giddy.

As I stepped into the yard, I heard Micky Jay's song 'the girl is mine' on the 'akasanoma' radio. I chuckled! Micky Jay was a very popular musician in Ash Town. Most of the girls from school thought that they were in love with him. They loved the sound of his voice.

It wasn't until much later that I learned that Micky's real name was Michael Jackson.

As I was getting ready to head out to the neighborhood, Mama beckoned me to her room. Her dead serious facial expression spoke volumes. I knew we were about to have an important talk. My mind was racing… Mama was about to talk about puberty! I told myself to calm down. I wasn't ready for the big talk.

When Mama started her speech, she was beating about the bush. She talked a lot about how beautiful I was and how much she treasured me. She talked about the bright future that lay ahead of me.

Eventually, she didn't have a choice but to tell me the real reason behind our conversation. She was about to ship me off to the big city as a maid.

Mama's second hand business was not doing well. The 1983 economic crisis had affected sales. A lot of her customers owed her money. For the past few months she hadn't been able to visit the big city to pick up a consignment. Money was tight.

The situation was even worse than I thought. Mama owed her Accra supplier a ton of money. She was yet to pay for the last 3 consignments. Mama and Dada were looking for ways to pay off their debts.

Unknown to me, my parents had been contemplating sending me off to work in Accra. As a maid, my salary was going to help them pay off their debt.

Mama made it sound as if moving to Accra as a maid was the greatest opportunity ever! She said I was going to the big city to help a rich family that lived in a mansion. She told me that I will be able to eat in a real plate and watch colored television. She said that I will have the opportunity to go to a very good school and also learn a trade.

The idea that I was going to Accra to learn a trade sounded really good. Mama said if I moved to the big city, my new madam could help me open my own hairdressing salon or help me become a big time seamstress.

She neglected to tell me that she had a preexisting relationship with my soon to be madam. See, she was about to ship me off to her second hand clothes supplier!

Oh, the illusions of the grand life as translated by a 12-year-old.

Somehow I was very excited? At that time, I thought it was like the best birthday gift ever. Me, going to live in a big mansion in Accra!

I could envision the good life. I didn't even realize that I was going to miss my family. I was excited about the opportunity that lay ahead.

However, as the evening drew closer, images of life in the city began to sink in. How much housework lay ahead of me? Were the promises true?

Several people had gone to Accra as maidservants and run back home to Ash Town. I had heard stories about how other kids my age had been mistreated by their employers. Was my madam going to be one of those wicked bosses?

Despite my misgivings, I was hopeful about the future. I believed that Mama had done her due diligence and that all will be well.

Before long, we started preparing for my journey to Accra.

My four mothers went to Kejetia market and bought a few pounds of meat and chicken. Together with my sisters, we cooked my going away feast. It felt like we were preparing for Christmas.

My family hadn't cooked such a big meal since the 1983 famine.

I remember cracking big city jokes with my sisters during the meal prep. With our limited English vocabulary, we pretended to be big Madams living in the big city. We gave instructions to our imaginary maids and acted like the rich people that we saw on TV.

For my going away party, we invited several neighbors and family members. It was a joyous occasion! We danced and laughed in the courtyard. I was on my way to the big city! In my mind, a better life lay ahead.

For a 12-year-old, the only downside to my relocation was me leaving Jahel behind. Oh, how my heart yearned for that boy who did not even know of my affection! I was definitely going to come back to Kumasi to marry Jahel.

The night before I left for Accra was an advice galore. The mothers sat me down to counsel me about my future. They cautioned me about the importance of abstinence, respect and hard work. They cautioned me to listen to my madam and not disgrace them.

That night, my family held a prayer meeting in my honor. Each person, young and old, prayed for my success. Mama said I was her hope and aspirations.

By the time we finished praying, the tears were flowing. Oh my goodness, I didn't think that I could have felt any sadder than I felt that evening.

We cried and hugged each other. Even Dada had tears in his eyes when he shook my hand.

PART II

THE

IN BETWEEN

JOURNEY TO ACCRA

JOURNEY TO ACCRA

Early Saturday morning, we boarded a trotro to the Neoplan bus station. By noon, we were on the big bus, on our way to Accra. I recall the ride being quite enjoyable. The bus was air-conditioned and I had a big seat.

About midway through the journey, we made a stop at Nkawkaw, an Eastern town. The driver's mate told us we had 30 minutes to use the restroom, eat, purchase items or do whatever we wished. The 30 minutes felt like forever. I was in a hurry to get to Accra.

There were several street vendors with artifacts and foodstuff by the roadside. Mama thought it'd be a good idea to buy a gift for my new madam. After bargaining with a plantain and yam seller, we were able to purchase two plantain bunches and 4 tubers of yam. We also bought some roasted corn and coconut for lunch.

Before long, the bus was back on the road. I don't remember much about the rest of the journey to Accra because I fell asleep during the second half of the trip.

It was late afternoon when we arrived at the Accra Neoplan Station. I had never seen that many buses. The station was bustling with lots of activities.

We picked up our belongings and headed towards the Circle Bus Terminal. It seemed like a lot of the people were walking fast or running. However, it was harder for us to pick up our pace. Not only did we have to carry our bags, we also had to transport the foodstuff that we bought at Nkawkaw.

In spite of our slow pace, we made it to the trotro line in good time. However, the mate told us that we had too many items for the trip and that we had to find a taxi to our destination. Ei, how were we going to afford a taxi in the big city?

Although we were disappointed, we realized that the only way to get to my new home would be via taxi. Therefore, with our limited funds, we hailed a taxi to Dansoman, my new hometown.

Our drive to the house was uneventful. We shared the taxi with 2 other passengers, one in the front seat and the other in the back with us. The lady who sat in the back was not pleasant. She looked at us funny. It was as if, Mama and I had a foul scent. The lady looked disgusted. She did not want her body to touch mine. However, she didn't have a choice because I was in the middle seat.

We drove past several shops and signs before arriving at our destination. When we got to the junction that led to the house, we paid the driver, alighted, and walked the rest of the way. After about a five-minute walk, we arrived at the security gate of a huge house. I wondered how anybody could live in such a house. I thought that maybe there was a school or office in the building. The Taylors' house was a mansion.

The security guard greeted us and asked us if we were the family from Kumasi. Mama replied in the affirmative. The guard was excited. He was originally from Wenkyi but had lived in Ash Town before moving to Accra. We were excited to meet him. It was nice to know that he had walked the same streets in Ash Town. He opened the gate for us and let us into the compound.

I was astounded! I couldn't believe my eyes. The house was even more beautiful than I had ever dreamed off. The doors were made of glass. I had never seen anything like that before.

When we entered the compound, a young man was working in the front garden. The security guard, whose name was Mr. Banda told the young man to let madam know that we had arrived. The young man invited us to walk with him to the front porch. He offered us a seat and then he went around the house to inform madam about our arrival.

My heart started to beat fast. Will my madam like me? What will I do when Mama leaves? My eyes started glistening. Mama was about to leave me with complete strangers. What lay ahead?

As I was getting lost in my thoughts, a pretty lady in a blue dress opened the door leading to the porch. She had the sincerest smile and the most beautiful eyes. She looked like she had just stepped off a movie set. Her braids were beautiful and her teeth glistened when she smiled.

As soon as we saw her, Mama stood up. ‘Auntie Aggie ooo”, as Mama stretched her arms, Auntie Aggie approached her with the widest embrace. They both said “atuuu.”

I was pleasantly surprised! I did not realize that Mama had such an amicable relationship with my madam. Apparently, Auntie Aggie owned one of the companies that supplied Mama with second hand clothing. Over the years they had become acquainted with each other. The friendly embrace between my mom and madam helped put me at ease.

Auntie Aggie looked at me, smiled, and said “Obaa Yaa, what a beautiful young girl. Welcome to Accra and to our home.” My heart melted. The madam said I was beautiful. I grinned from ear to ear. Thank you, madam, I responded eagerly.

Without hesitation, Auntie Aggie told me that she'd rather I call her Auntie. And just like that, I had begun to bond with my new boss.

After exchanging pleasantries, Auntie welcomed me formally to the household. She told me that so far as I did what was required of me I was going to be fine. I was quite happy when she informed me that I will be starting the local public school in September of that year. She called out to Awo (her other house help) and told her to go and show me my room. I picked up my bags and followed Awo towards the back of the house. Mama and Auntie Aggie continued their conversation.

Awo was full of smiles. She even offered to help me with the bags. I did not have much to carry so I just held on to my luggage. The servant's quarters were at the very back of the house. The Taylors called the living quarters the boys' quarters. As we entered the quarters, I realized that it was bigger than our home in Kumasi. We had our own kitchen, bathroom and living room. We even had a colored television and a big radio. Well, I thought it was a radio. I didn't realize it was a cassette player. I hadn't even seen that before.

Awo led me to our room. I had my own bed and it had already been laid. I was blown away. As I watched Awo, I wondered how old she was. It was too soon to ask her personal questions. She looked old enough to be my big sister.

Later that week, I found out that Awo was 16 years old. She had been living with Auntie Aggie and her family for the past 5 years. Not only was Awo smart, she had aced her O'level exams. Just as I was going to be starting a new school in September, Awo was also getting ready to enroll in sixth form.

After putting my bags away, I walked back to the main house to say my goodbyes to Mama.

By allowing me to serve as a maid, Auntie Aggie decided to write off Mama's consignment debt. In addition to forgiving the debt, Auntie Aggie paid Mama an advance on my service.

I was happy for my family. Grateful that I had contributed to their well-being.

Before long, it was time for Mama to leave. Auntie Aggie surprised us all when she instructed her driver to drop Mama off at the Circle Neoplan bus station. At least Mama didn't have to pay another lorry fare. I hugged my Mama tight. I couldn't help the tears that trickled down my face. Mama was headed back to Kumasi without me.

I was about to embark on a new chapter of my life.

As I lay in bed that night, I wondered about my family. What were my siblings up to? Were they missing me? I wish they could see my foam bed. I was no longer sleeping on a floor mat with my sisters.

Although I was sharing a bedroom with Awo, I had my own bed. Through the dark, I could still see traces of the curtains in the room. I couldn't believe my luck. I was thankful for the opportunity to be living in this big house. I promised myself that I would make my parents proud. Lost in my thoughts, I drifted to sleep.

CHANGE

CHANGE

Obaa Yaa, Obaa Yaa, Obaa Yaa - the women were screaming my name. I wondered if I had done something wrong. Then I saw their angry faces. They were definitely upset with me. One of them lifted her hand to smack me, but I dodged her. Then another came lunging at me! I picked myself up and began running for dear life.

The roads were unfamiliar. I didn't know where I was headed, but I kept going. I was panting. I did not want the women to catch up with me. Then out of nowhere, one of them grabbed my shoulders and started shaking me.

I started begging her. I was crying… and she called out my name – Obaa Yaa, Obaa Yaa.

Then, I opened my eyes. Awo was standing over me. Calling out my name. She was trying to wake me up for my morning chores.

Then it hit me. It was all a dream. My pillow was wet and there were tears streaming down my face. I had been crying in my sleep. Awo consoled me and told me that I was going to be okay.

It was my first morning away from home and I wanted to do everything by the book. Thanks to Awo, I knew my chores and responsibilities.

There were a few surprises in store for me. For example, using the bathroom was different at the Taylor household. We had a commode at the boys' quarters so I didn't have to worry about squatting or any of the 'who dey for top' business.

Excitedly, I stepped into the bathroom to do a no. 2. As I evaluated the commode, I realized that it was different from our outhouse back home. The commode was as clean as a whistle.

It felt really good to take care of business. I didn't have to deal with any flies or splashes! But then, I when I finished easing myself, I wasn't sure about the next steps. The shank was still floating in there. I thought it would have just gone down the drain.

I didn't realize that I needed to use the handle on the side to flush everything down. Luckily for me, Awo came to the rescue. She showed me how the commode worked. I was fortunate to have Awo.

Infact, my early days at the Taylor house were very different from what I was used to. We even had an indoor shower and a fancy stove at the boys' quarters. Despite hearing stories about the fancy life in the big city, I was in total awe of the Taylors' wealth. Fancy plates, glasses, furniture, televisions – you name it!

REALITY

REALITY

Two months into my job, Auntie enrolled me at the local public school. It wasn't until I started school that I began to feel the pressures of being a maid. Combining my housework with school was not easy. The school work was harder than I anticipated. Unfortunately, nobody was available to help me review homework.

As much as I didn't mind doing chores, I began to resent the Taylor kids. Here I was, living in a house with kids my age, who considered me their personal maid. I cleaned their rooms, served their guests and even run errands for their friends. I knew I was being paid for my job but it irked me that I had to clean up after them.

The Taylor kids did not pick up after themselves. I felt like it was my responsibility to take care of their whims and everything in between.

I began to question my parents' motives for bringing me to Accra. Although I was grateful that I lived in a nice house, I missed my family. I realized that although we may have been poor, I was happier back home.

As the days dragged by, I began studying for my secondary school exams. I knew my options were limited and that my job required for me to be a day student at a nearby school. I would study late into the night because I was determined to make a better life for myself.

Studying at night wasn't easy. There were times when my mind will drift off - wondering how my family was doing back home. Although my employers had telephones, nobody called to check on me.

Well, it wasn't that simple. My family did not have a home phone. They could have probably called from a communication center but I doubt if they had the phone number to Auntie's house.

I thought about my family a lot. I missed the nights under the mango tree. Every night as I lay in bed, I will pray for God's protection on my entire family. Most of all, I prayed for a visit from Mama.

MAMA VISITS

MAMA VISITS

The Christmas holidays were drawing closer and the Taylor household was bustling with activity. The excitement about the holidays was contagious. Visitors streamed in and out of the house throughout the day. Several Taylor relatives stopped by to collect their yearly stipend.

Awo and I helped bake cakes and pastries for Auntie's friends. As a result of our baking fiesta, the kitchen had a sweet aroma.

The work was nonstop. After Auntie showed me the recipe for her baked goods, most of the prep work fell on my shoulders. I had to mix the margarine and sugar for the pound cake by hand. And, I had to bake over 20 pounds of cake!! It was not an easy feat! My hands were feeling sore by the end of the third day.

However, there was a lot of excitement in the air so I didn't have the time to complain.

The Taylors received lots of Christmas cards and gifts from their family members. I realized that the rich Accra people celebrated the holidays differently.

Back home in Ash Town, we did not send or receive cards. The well wishes and festivities were enough. We mostly celebrated with food, music and dancing. Some years we were lucky to receive second hand clothes or shoes from our parents.

Usually, the shoe or dress will be a slightly bigger size in anticipation of a growth spurt during the year. It was interesting to see the contrast between my family and the Taylors.

Despite the numerous gifts and activities at the Taylors, the children were not satisfied. They wanted more expensive things.
The kids complained about their gifts. They didn't even realize that they were lucky and blessed to receive that many gifts from their parents.

The best day out of the holiday season was December 26th. That was the day that I received gifts from the Taylors. I was very appreciative because I had never received a wrapped gift in my life. When we woke up that morning, the Taylors had left a big 'Ghana must go' bag on our porch. The bag was filled with wrapped gifts.

I received dresses, shoes, a bag and a Walkman. I couldn't believe that I was that lucky. I didn't even realize that my gifts were repackaged goods. The Taylor kids had re gifted the stuff that they did not want.

Well, I did not mind at all. It was okay with me. I loved the gifts. If only I could share my dresses with my sisters, it would have been perfect.

As if God could hear my thoughts, Awo came running to the boy's quarters. She was all smiles. I had a guest at the gate!

Mama had arrived with tubers of yam and plantains. She had traveled to Accra to see how I was adjusting to my new environment. It was very nice of Mama to bring the Taylors a gift. I was overjoyed to see her. As she hugged me, Mama said, "Obaa Yaa, me broni."

All the emotions were threatening to erupt. The tears streamed down my face. I was homesick. I couldn't help it. I begged Mama to take me back home. Her heart was heavy but she did not give in.

Our moment together was brief. I didn't even get to talk to Mama much. She spent most of her visit on the main house porch waiting for Auntie Aggie. As a maid, I could not wait with her, I had to get back to my chores.

After about an hour, I was summoned to the porch. We exchanged a few pleasantries and I said bye to my Mama.

MOVING FORWARD

MOVING FORWARD

The year was 1985 and changes were on the horizon. I had qualified to attend Wesley Grammar School. Auntie and Awo were very proud of me.

However, my fortunes were about to change. As we were preparing for my secondary school transition Auntie received news that her sister's family were about to relocate to America.

One late afternoon in April, Auntie invited Awo and I to the main house for a talk. She told us that her sister, Auntie Mary, and family, had received an offer to go and work as diplomats in America. Auntie Mary's husband, Mr. Abban was going to work at the American Embassy in New York.

Auntie Mary (Abban) had asked to take Awo to America to help with her business. However,

Auntie (Aggie) did not think it was a good time for Awo to leave because of her upcoming A' levels.

Rather, Auntie had suggested that her sister take me instead. She thought it'd be a good opportunity for me. She informed me that my parents had already agreed to the proposal.

Auntie's words sounded like a dream. Me? Going to America? Whaat! Unbelievable! My fortunes were about to change.

I was going to the land where everybody was successful. I was thrilled about the possibility of going to America. And I was certain that Mama was elated too.

This was great news. Not only was I going to help Auntie Mary with her business, but I would also have the opportunity to go to an American school.

We began preparing feverishly for my trip with The Abbans.

In order to help pay for my portion of the trip, Dada sold the family property in our village to a local businessman recommended by Auntie Mary.

Unbeknownst to my family, the Abbans had a deal with the so called businessman. They turned around and resold the land for much more.

Dada probably didn't care about the shady portion of the deal. My family wanted to invest in me. They believed that my life in America was going to be a good return on their investment. One day, I was going to lift my family out of poverty.

Before our trip, Auntie Mary took me to a big pink house for my travel papers. When we arrived at the house, a man in a blue shirt took a picture of me. He said it was for my passport. Then I was told about my new name. For purposes of traveling to America, I was going to be called Yvonne Abban. My passport had my new name. I did not understand why I had to change my name but Auntie Mary assured me that I could only travel to America under a different name.

Auntie Aggie and her family were sad to see me go. However, they assured me that it was for the best. After all, I was going to live with their family.

Mama came to visit one last time before I left for America.

PART III

TODAY

AMERICA

AMERICA

I couldn't believe that I was traveling to America. My life was definitely about to change for the better. I was a very lucky girl. Auntie Mary had coached me on what to say to the immigration officials. My name was Yvonne Abban and I was her niece.

Basically, I was leaving Sasha and my whole identity behind. At that time, I didn't realize that Auntie Mary and her family had me traveling on somebody else's passport.

They had given me a different date of birth and a whole new identity in order to bring me to America.

When we arrived at the Kotoka airport, we were escorted to the VIP lounge. Because of the Abbans' political appointment, we didn't have to go through strenuous immigration procedures.

After about 2 hours at the airport, we boarded the Delta flight to America.

I was scared to be traveling on the big bird. There were times that the plane shook. At that time, I didn't know what turbulence was. I was scared that we could crash. I remained seated throughout the flight. I didn't want to risk walking around. My heart was basically sitting in my stomach for hours.

Oh, and there was this inquisitive lady sitting next to me on the flight. She badgered me with questions! "Where are you from?" "Who are you traveling with?" "Where are you going?" It felt like an unending slew of questions. When she asked about the whereabouts of my family. I told her that Auntie Mary was sitting in one of the seats upfront.

Yes. Auntie and the rest of the family traveled by business class while I sat in coach. I didn't know the difference. I was just happy to be on a plane traveling to America. The flight lasted all night. By morning, we arrived in New York.

Going through immigration was a breeze. Back then, customs did not have complicated biometric machines. They did not detect that I was traveling on another person's passport. Maybe my ignorance helped. I did not know that I was committing a crime. I just assumed that it was okay to travel as someone else.

After going through customs at JFK airport, a delegation from the Ghana embassy met us and drove us to the Abbans' future home.

As we drove through the streets of New York, I couldn't help but to marvel at all the cars on the road.

I didn't see any of the boneshakers that I was used to traveling in. Even the buses looked very nice on the outside. I looked around for street hawkers but to my surprise, there were none on the roads. The ride was smooth. No bumpy roads. America was beautiful! All the cars stayed in their lanes and traveled in the same direction. Eishhh, America was nice.

It took us a while to get to our destination. As we got closer to home, I realized that there were less cars on the road. It also seemed that we were leaving the taller buildings behind. Other than Auntie giving me instructions, nobody really talked to me during the ride from JFK to the house.

Within an hour, we arrived at our destination. As we dragged our luggage inside, I thought about the adventure that lay ahead. I was going to become a student in America. And one day, I was going to be rich!

When I entered the house, I was surprised at the size. The Taylor house in Ghana was much bigger than this New York house. We didn't have a gate like the Accra house. Even the rooms seemed smaller.

Despite the smaller house, Auntie Mary and her kids were very excited.

As I stood there wondering about my sleeping quarters, Auntie asked me to follow her down the stairs. Lo and behold, there was a room under the house! I did not realize that people could live underground. Ei, America!

Auntie told me that the area was called a basement and that I was going to be living there. You are probably thinking that I was lucky to have the basement to myself right?

Well, the only problem was that, the space wasn't completely finished. Also, it was dusty, and there were no windows.

I did not have a bed either. I wondered why I would come to America to sleep on the floor in a dusty room. Would I not have been better off being a maid in Ghana?

I began to wonder what my true fate was going to be. I had a deep sense of foreboding. This was not the American life that I had seen on TV! As the sadness crept in, I told myself that Auntie was a very nice woman and that she will make sure that I was okay.

WELCOME FOR REAL

WELCOME FOR REAL

I spent the first few days cleaning my room and making my space habitable. Auntie gave me an air mattress. Although it was summer, the basement was not hot. It was bearable. I will only begin to feel the extreme cold when winter rolled around.

We had been in America for about a month and I had never set foot outside our home. My role was to do chores around the house and to stay in the basement whenever I wasn't needed upstairs.

The nature of my chores varied. Although I was responsible for the cleaning and laundry, I also baked meat pie, chips, and made shito (black pepper) for Auntie's customers. I was Auntie's official housekeeper and chef.

The Abban kids were already settled into their routines. One of them was getting ready for college and the other two were enrolled in high school.

As a thirteen-year-old, I should have been enrolled in middle school but Auntie told me that we didn't have all the paperwork for my enrollment. Who was I to doubt my benefactor? I believed in Auntie and was hopeful that I was going to enroll in school one day.

The months went by. Soon it was my first American Thanksgiving. I spent days cooking and baking for auntie's clients. Whenever I wasn't in the kitchen, I was either engaged in another household chore or cooped up in the basement.

I'm not even sure if I knew or understood what Thanksgiving was about. The day came and went without much incident.

I helped with the prepping of the meals. However, when it was time to eat, I was relegated to the basement.

Christmas was no different. Unlike Christmas in Accra where I received gifts from Auntie Aggie and her family, Auntie Mary did not include me in the American festivities.

I was baffled. I didn't know what to do. I wish I hadn't come to America. I sat in the basement crying. I was missing my family. And I had no way of contacting them. My parents did not have an address or phone number. I did not know Auntie Aggie's address either. It was like I had been cut off from the rest of the world. I spent my days laboring for Auntie Mary and her family.

The brutal winter didn't help my predicament. My room in the basement did not have any heat. I had many a sleepless night because of the cold weather.

I will wear layers of clothing under my jacket before going to bed.

When I realized that my situation was not going to improve, I devised a plan to escape from Auntie Mary's house. I was going to run away.

FILLA

FILLA

I knew I wanted to leave Auntie Mary's house but I wasn't sure where I was going. Not only was I penniless but also, I did not have any relatives or know anybody in America. What in the world was I going to do? Any strategy was going to require some craftiness on my part.

Maybe a church will take me in? Maybe I'll meet a good Samaritan? I just couldn't quite figure out how to put a plan in motion.

As I mulled over my plans, fate had a different plan in the works.

There was another government reshuffle in Ghana. This time, Mr. Abban was not so lucky. He lost his job.

Since the house came with the job, the family was required to move out. The Abbans didn't have a choice but to find temporary housing and 'papers' or move back to Ghana.

As a result of the Government reshuffle and possible move, Auntie decided to take me on some of her errands. She needed me to help carry large items to her car. One of the errands was to the African store in the Bronx.

It was exciting being in a store with so many other Africans. Several people were speaking the local language. People were smiling and everybody seemed nice. I thought to myself that maybe one of the people at the store will take me in and I wouldn't have to go back to Ghana without accomplishing anything in America.

Then out of the blue I heard him.

“Ei, Mr. Ampadu, do you have alata samina?” The voice sounded so familiar. I didn’t want to believe it. Could that be a voice from Kumasi?

Curiously, I turned around. Oh my God, I couldn’t believe it. Standing in front of me was my cousin Bro. Kwabena the teacher! Remember Bro. Kwabena who used to teach my siblings and I in Kumasi? Yes, Bro. Kwabena was in America.

I jumped and screamed his name! “Obaa Yaa, what are you doing in America?” Bro. Kwabena asked.

I told him that I was staying with Auntie Mary and that we were scheduled to move back to Ghana soon. Bro. Kwabena was very happy to see me.

Apparently, he had bought a green card from a family and relocated to America. He was a tutor at a learning center.

I was over the moon. I wondered if I could go and live with Bro. Kwabena. I felt as if this was an intervention from God. Before we left the store, Bro. Kwabena wrote his phone number on a piece of paper and handed it to me. He also gave his number to Auntie Mary.

On the ride back home, I couldn't help but smile. Was this God's way of making a way for me in America? I mean I had been cooped up in the house all these months. The first day that Auntie takes me to the African store, I meet a relative.

When we got home, I helped Auntie offload her items from the car. I wanted to be on the best behavior.

After my evening chores, I gathered the courage to talk to her about the possibility of me staying in America. I pleaded with her that I did not want to go back to Ghana yet.

Surprisingly, her heart was softened. Or maybe she didn't want me going back home to tell Auntie Aggie how I had been maltreated.

Auntie Mary okayed my stay in America if I could find someone to live with.

I was fourteen years old.

MOVING ON

MOVING ON

I bet you are thinking about my next move. And you are convinced that I contacted Bro. Kwabena? Well, that's true.

That evening, Auntie allowed me to use the house phone to call the only family I knew in America.

With much trepidation, I dialed Bro. Kwabena's number. He sounded tired when he picked up the phone. I explained my current situation to him and asked if I could move in with him and enroll in school.

I shared my residency fears with him. I was wondering how I could stay if Auntie and her family moved back to Ghana. By then, I knew that I didn't have the right 'papers' to stay in America. I wondered if there was a way to get some American papers. I had no idea how long it was going to take to become a true legal resident of Yankey.

Bro. Kwabena laid my fears to rest. He invited me to come live with him. He sounded optimistic over the phone.

After our conversation, Bro. Kwabena asked to speak to Auntie. I passed the phone to her. I was excited. Finally, I was going to experience the real America.

Two days later, Bro. Kwabena picked me up. I didn't have much to pack. My things fit in the one suitcase that I brought to America.

As I was leaving the Abbans, I knew that nobody was sorry to see me go. I wasn't going to be missed. It felt like I was never wanted in the first place.

Our trip from White Plains to the Bronx lasted about three hours. We spent 25 minutes waiting for our first bus. We had several stops along the way.

We traveled via the Westchester County - Bee Line System to Mamaroneck Avenue. Then we took another bus from Mamaroneck Avenue to Mosholu Parkway. After we got off, we walked to my new home at Tracy Towers.

Bro. Kwabena was renting a bedroom from one of the residents. I didn't mind sleeping on the floor. I was just happy to find a relative in America.

YANKEY GIRL

YANKEY GIRL

When I left the Abbans, Auntie did not hand over my ‘Yvonne’ papers.

As a result, I had no record of having entered America. We were in a dilemma. How could I enroll in school?

Although Bro. Kwabena had a green card, he couldn’t file for me because I had already entered the country. Besides, I was his cousin so the process wouldn’t have worked.

To help me transition into the American system, he called a few of his friends who had helped immigrants in the past. Within two weeks my paper situation was resolved. At least, I thought so!

Bro. Kwabena's friend created a green card for me. With my new identification, I was ready to enroll in school.

After some diligent research, we decided that it will be best for me to enroll at Bronx Science. However, we had to hold back because I did not have a transcript or the score for the application process.

I was fortunate to have Bro. Kwabena's guidance. He was familiar with the educational system and knew that my best option was to enroll in middle school.

In the fall, I got my first taste of the American education. I enrolled as an eighth grader at Bronx Middle.

TRANSITION

TRANSITION

I was very excited about my first day of school in America. The weekend before school started, we went to Walmart to buy all my supplies. I woke up early on Monday morning to catch the school bus.

That morning, I wore my brand new Salvation Army jacket. I also had brand new shoes from Payless.

I hummed to myself as I walked towards the bus stop. Although it was a cold morning, I arrived early. I didn't want to risk missing the bus.

I was one of the first people in line when the bus pulled up. When I hopped on, I realized that the bus was half full. I said hello to the driver and walked down the aisle to find a seat.

Riding on the school bus was a nightmare. Nobody wanted me to sit next to them. People put bags next to their seats as I walked through the bus. They had saved the spots for their friends. When I approached the back of the bus, I saw a girl in a red jacket smiling at me. I seized the opportunity to ask if I could sit next to her. Luckily, she obliged.

I introduced myself when I sat down but she didn't want to talk much. After a few pleasantries, I followed her cue and rode quietly to school.

My first day at school was not exciting. I felt clueless and alone. Most of the kids had known each other since 6th grade. It was hard to make friends.

The next few weeks were difficult. I walked the halls of Bronx Middle with such trepidation. Although there were a lot people who looked like me, I just didn't fit in. It was hard communicating

with the other kids. Their favorite words to me were "say what?"
Middle school was not what I had expected. Here I was, a new girl from Africa with a thick accent and no friends. During lunchtime, I sat in the corner with my food. The other immigrant children wouldn't even talk to me.

I wondered what was wrong with me. I knew how to braid my hair nicely so it wasn't like I looked unkempt. Although, I did not have a variety of clothes, my outfits were clean. There were times that I wondered if I smelled funny. Because people will make faces and sounds when I walked by.

Adjusting to the American school system was harder than I thought. My eighth grade experience was unpleasant. I didn't make new friends or participate in any extracurricular activities. My life was pretty much home, school, and back home.

During the school year, I took the entry exam for Bronx Science. I was hopeful that my high school experience will be better.

Finding out that I had been accepted was the highlight of my summer. I couldn't wait to enroll!

However, in the summer of 1987, Bro. Kwabena received a job offer from the PG County school system in Maryland.

The offer was his best yet. He was over the moon. It was time to live his American dream. As fate will have it, my plans of going to Bronx High will not materialize because we had to move to Maryland.

It didn't take long to realize that the pace of life in Maryland was not as hectic as New York.

We found a nice one-bedroom apartment in Bowie.

Compared to our room in New York, our Maryland apartment was a castle!

In the fall, I enrolled at Bowie High.

Ninth grade was not what I had anticipated. Despite me being a new student, I did not feel alienated. There were a few friendly students in my grade.

Overall, life in Maryland was off to a good start. Bro. Kwabena was good to me. He treated me like a little sister. Finally, I began to assimilate into my new culture.

By 10th grade, my English had improved and I was confident to run for class president. I don't even know why I thought I was ready for student leadership.

Maybe I was overly confident. It wasn't surprising when I received less than 5% of the votes. But hey, that wasn't too bad. The votes showed that there were classmates who believed in me. It made me realize that I was capable of pursuing my dreams.

BAMBI

BAMBI

Have you ever been in that situation where someone or something disrupts your plans? Well, that happened when Bambi showed up in Bro. Kwabena's life.

During our New York days, Bro. Kwabena had been focused on landing the big job so he didn't have a lot of time for relationships.

Maryland was a different ball game. Now, he had the job and a nice apartment! It was just a matter of time for a lady to make her way into Bro. Kwabena's life.

First, it was the phone calls. Every evening, she would call and ask to speak to Bro. Kwabena. She introduced herself as Bambi. Over the phone she sounded nice. I liked her. Then she started visiting. Before I knew it, she was spending more time at the apartment. By my junior year, Bambi was basically living with us.

Then things began to change. There was a new boss in town. I was no longer the ‘woman’ of the house. BAMBI took over the kitchen and the living room. She placed pictures of her and Bro. Kwabena around the house.

Basically, I felt like a guest in the apartment. Sometimes she will be sprawled in the sofa when I got home from school. Since we had one sofa in the apartment, there was nowhere for me to sit.

Unfortunately, I couldn’t hang out in the bedroom either. My only refuge was the kitchen. Life became uncomfortable, but Bro. Kwabena hardly noticed.

It was tough.

Luckily for me I had started working at the McDonalds close to our apartment.

Every evening, after my shift, I will just hang out at work to finish my homework. At that point, a part of me wished that I lived on my own, but I didn't have the money. Besides, I was an 11th grader. It made much more sense to stay with my family.

OBLIGATIONS

&

DOUBTS

OBLIGATIONS & DOUBTS

In the meantime, the relatives in Ghana had the home phone number. Every now and then, they will call us collect from Ghana. It seemed that they either asked for money or delivered news of a death in the family.

It wasn't too long before I had to start sending money home on a monthly basis. I didn't have time to hang out with friends or do regular teenage stuff. I had responsibilities.

As other students began discussing their college aspirations, the reality hit me. I needed some form of financial aid or scholarship for college. Was I even going to qualify? How was I going to handle the application process?

I mean, my green card wasn't even real. What if the colleges found out that my 'papers' were fake?

One thing was for sure. Me, I was going to go to college. I didn't know how. But I knew I had to make it work.

My junior year was full of uncertainty. I didn't feel like I had a home and I had no idea what the future looked like.

But I promised myself, I was going to find a way!

ENCOUNTERS

ENCOUNTERS

The summer before 12th grade, I found a better paying job away from home. One of the ladies at church told me about an agency that was hiring live-in care workers. Luckily for me, the agency was not too stringent with its hiring practices. I walked in there one afternoon, filled out the forms and received a call back the next day.

They had found a job for me in Silver Spring. My job was to take care of an elderly woman in her apartment. The good part, I was required to stay with the woman.

This was great news. I could escape from Bro. Kwabena and Bambi for a minute!

I packed my bags and left for my summer home. I thought to myself, how hard could it be? Taking care of someone's needs at home did not sound like a strenuous job. After all, I used to be a maid servant.

I was right. The live-in job was even easier than I anticipated.

My boss' name was Ms. Mary. She was a pleasant widow who needed companionship. I fixed her meals, bathed her, helped her dress and made sure that she was taking her medication.

I was responsible for scheduling her doctor appointments because her memory was not that great. Ms. Mary had an early onset of dementia and had suffered a stroke two years prior.

There were days that she would forget who I was and what I was doing in her house. However, the days that she remembered me, compensated for all the other bad days. Ms. Mary was a very pleasant woman. I enjoyed staying with her.

The August before school started, Ms. Mary's son came to visit. His name was Lamar. Prior to his visit I had been giving him progress reports over the phone.

Lamar was nice. He asked me about my background and talked to me like I mattered.

I was nineteen years old and had never dated anyone. I kind of liked Lamar.

GOOD NEWS

GOOD NEWS

Just before the beginning of my 12th grade year, I moved back home. My live-in gig was cut short because of the fall semester.

I had to go back to my McDonalds job. I wish I could have stayed at Ms. Mary's but there was no way I could be a live-in caregiver and attend school every day.

Bro. Kwabena was happy to have me back. He even made time to play 'ludu' with me. We introduced Bambi to the game. She loved it. Surprisingly, I became more tolerant of Bambi. Maybe I had been jealous earlier because Bro. Kwabena wasn't spending as much time with me as before.

It looked like we were finally getting into a new family routine. I started looking forward to Bambi's pork chops! She liked to cook on Sundays.

Bro. Kwabena continued to encourage me to invest more time into my education. As a result, I became more laser-focused on school. It was time to apply for college.

The Bowie High counselors were helpful with the decision process. They advised me to apply to a community college because of my grades and financial situation. Since I didn't have a high GPA, my options were limited.

I applied to Montgomery Community College. My heart was in my stomach as I waited to hear back from the admissions department.

When I was researching about tuition rates, I realized that my tuition was going to be lower if I was a resident of Montgomery County. So I decided to get crafty. I used Ms. Mary's Silver Spring address for my application. I was just hoping that the college wouldn't ask too many questions and that they wouldn't find out that I was a PG County resident.

To make sure that my Montgomery County residency was legit, I applied for a state ID at the DMV with Ms. Mary's address. Luckily for me, I had received mail from the agency at Ms. Mary's house so I had a proof of address. I had covered the basis. I just needed to get in.

On a cold Monday evening in February, I received a phone call from Lamar. He told me about the Montgomery County envelope that he had picked up from his Mama's house. My heart missed a beat. That night, Lamar drove to my job with the envelope.

My hands shook as I opened the envelope. My heart was beating so fast. It felt like something was going to happen to me. I was calling on the angels in my head. I pulled the letter out. And there it was! I had received admission to Montgomery College. I was elated. Lamar seemed happy for me too!

I couldn't wait to get home and share my good news with Bro. Kwabena!

NOT APRIL FOOL

NOT APRIL FOOL

As I walked home that night, I hummed to myself. I thought about Mama and my siblings. I was going to become somebody in America. I couldn't wait to share my news with Bro. Kwabena! Like him, I was going to be in a position to help our relatives. Oh Yankey! The dream was about to come true.

Then I arrived at our apartment complex. From a distance, I could see two police cars parked in front of our apartment building. I wondered who they could be visiting.

Then, I heard the sound of the ambulance. Ei, was somebody sick? The ambulance drove right past me.

I stepped to the side because I didn't want to get in the way. I saw a policeman come out of our building. The EMS people rushed into the building.

I was confused. I wanted to go inside. But then, I was afraid. What if the police discovered that I didn't have paper?

Then I saw Bambi. She was running behind the EMS people. She looked distraught.

Oh my God! What could be wrong? Ei!! God help me ooo. I recognized the Abedi Pele t-shirt on the stretcher. Jesus don't come. What was wrong with Bro. Kwabena?

My brain was about to explode! My heart was going to jump out of my body. Bambi was incoherent. She said Bro. Kwabena wasn't breathing.

I ran to the ambulance. I started screaming! Bro Kwabena! Bro. Kwabena! Please wake up wae. Bro. Kwabena, please wake up oo. Ei Awurade! I told the EMS that I was his sister.

I don't even know how we made it to the hospital. Bro. Kwabena had accidentally ingested peanuts. How could this happen?

Bro Kwabena was very cautious with his eating habits. He hardly ate out because of his peanut allergy.

Apparently, Bro Kwabena had eaten peanut butter cookies without knowing that the ingredients included peanuts. Unfortunately, they could not find Bro. Kwabena's EpiPen after he ingested the cookies so he went into acute respiratory distress.

Bro. Kwabena died that day. It was April 1.

My only relative in America was gone. I had nowhere to turn.

I couldn't even share my college acceptance news with my Bro. Kwabena.

I sat on the hospital floor. Wondering who I was going to call and what I was going to do.

I didn't know how to have a funeral.
The world was spinning.

ARRANGEMENTS

ARRANGEMENTS

The next few days were a blur. When I called the relatives in Ghana to inform them about Bro. Kwabena's demise, the wailing on the other end of the line was gut wrenching. A mighty tree had fallen. The future looked grim. Bro. Kwabena was a star in our family. Not only had he made it to America, but also he had a good job and took care of the family needs.

The conversation was heartbreaking. My family was devastated. They wanted me to bring Bro. Kwabena's body home for the funeral. Our culture believed in honoring the dead.

Unfortunately, there was no way I could make that trip back home without repercussions. I would have loved to go to Ghana but I couldn't risk it because l didn't have my papers. I probably would not have been able to reenter the United States if I had gone back home. There was no way around it. Bro. Kwabena had to be buried in America.

With help from our pastor and Bro. Kwabena's co-workers, we found a plot, bought a coffin and buried my cousin. I was actually surprised at the number of people at the service.

Back in Ash Town, funerals were a big deal. You could have anywhere from 600 to 2000 mourners at a funeral. Some of the people at the funerals did not know the deceased or have a connection with the family. People just showed up because of the refreshments or the possibility of finding a date.

Bro. Kwabena's American funeral was solemn. There was no wailing or theatrics. We had less than 50 people at the service.

The funeral home reserved the front row for family and close friends. I sat next to Bambi. She was my only family now.

I sat through the funeral wondering what was going to become of me. Where was I going to live till college? I hoped that Bambi wouldn't leave the apartment. I felt very much alone and sad. Bro. Kwabena was my guardian in America. He had helped me transition into my new life.

When it was my turn to read the tribute, I broke down. My tears were not just for Bro. Kwabena. I cried for myself. We didn't have any other relatives in America.

The pain in my heart was so weird. I had never been that sad.

The graveside was the toughest part. After the service, our pastor, Bambi, myself and one of Bro.

Kwabena's friends stayed behind to say our final goodbyes.

As they lowered the casket into the ground, I started shaking. I was cold all over. There was a presence at the burial grounds. Now that I think about it, I believe that there is some kind of spirituality to death.

I swear I felt Bro. Kwabena say bye to me at the graveside. I don't wish that feeling of vacuum on anyone. It was a very sad day.

After the graveside service, Bambi and I hugged each other tight. I felt like she was that one person who knew Bro. Kwabena well. Amidst tears, we said bye to each other.

Pastor had offered for me to stay with his family in Greenbelt for a few days. Together with Pastor's wife, we spent the next 2 days trying to figure out my future.

They were both happy to hear about my college admission. Their comforting words made me feel warm and fuzzy inside. At least, somebody cared about me. I was a few months from finishing 12th grade.

Pastor was very supportive but I couldn't stay with his family in their two-bedroom apartment because there was no room for me. They were a family of 6.

After 2 days, I headed back to our apartment. Pastor gave me a few phone cards, groceries and some spending money.

I was happy to find Bambi sitting in the living room when I entered the apartment. Maybe she will be like a sister to me, I thought. We chatted for a few minutes. We really didn't have much to say to each other. However, it was comforting to know that I was not alone in my grief.

Then came the time to provide the family with a status update. I picked up the phone. The $10 phone card was perfect for the multiple phone calls. First, I called the communication center to send word to remind the family about the upcoming call. When the family arrived at the' com center', they placed a collect call to me. As usual, I did not accept the call. That was the family's way of letting me know that they were waiting for my call. Right after I hang up, I called the 'com center'. The conversation that followed was one of the toughest conversations I'd ever had with my family.

The folks back home were very upset. They couldn't believe that we had buried Bro. Kwabena already. Mama and my aunties said we had buried him like a chicken. Although I explained the American culture to the family, they were adamant that we had disrespected Bro. Kwabena by burying him too soon.

As I listened to the family over the phone, I realized that they did not have any concept of my lonely state. They were assuming that because I was in America, I was probably okay.

My fears were buried in the pit of my stomach. Where would I live? What would I do?

AFTER

AFTER

I was impressed by the number of people who called to check on me during the first two weeks after Bro. Kwabena's funeral. However, after those first few weeks, it felt like the people were starting to forget about me. As they went back to their everyday routines, the frequency of calls started dwindling.

During those first few weeks, people offered to help with my needs. I believed them. I felt confident that the church members will step up and support me in my time of need. I didn't realize that most of the people were paying lip service. And that they will be full of excuses or may not even pick up my call in my time of need.

Through Bro. Kwabena's death, I learned the importance of being self-sufficient. After the first few weeks, it felt like I had hit a brick wall. My situation was just another story to be told. Maybe if we had been very active church members, it would have made a difference.

See, our church members did not know us that well. We were not one of the regulars so I wasn't entirely surprised when the phone calls stopped. Other than asking me how I was doing, the conversations seemed to be one-sided. I did not have much to say because I did not have a rapport with the people.

Bambi was a regular in my life. I looked forward to seeing her after work. I wasn't sure about our relationship. She hardly talked to me but I appreciated her presence.

Unfortunately for me, the companionship that Bambi provided did not last. By the end of April, Bambi moved out of the apartment. She just packed her bags and left one Sunday afternoon.

It was kind of emotional. Although we did not have a close relationship, I was sad to see her go. The day she left, she gave me a hug and $100 spending money.

A white Lexus picked her up from the apartment. When I walked her to the car, the man driving greeted me by bopping his head. Bambi had probably found a new boyfriend. The tears streamed down my face when I hugged her bye. I did not expect that level of sadness. Another chapter of my life had ended.

I shed more tears as I walked back to the apartment. For the first time since Bro. Kwabena died, I was truly alone.

I knew I had to make a decision about my living conditions. I could not afford the rent for the apartment. I needed to find a quick solution to avoid being kicked out by the landlord.

Bro. Kwabena had already paid the April rent so my plan was to find a solution before the beginning of May. Since I was going to graduate in May, my goal was to find a job in Montgomery County and maybe rent a room from someone. Ideally, I wanted to find a place close to school.

Right around this time, I reconnected with Lamar. He seemed like a good listener. Before long, the occasional phone calls turned into a daily ritual. By the time I graduated from high school, Lamar was a staple in my life. Lucky me, I had found a good friend.

GRADUATION

GRADUATION

May 25, 1992. It was the day that Jay Leno became the host of NBC's Tonight Show. That day, I graduated from high school.

As I walked in the procession, my eyes welled with tears. If only this graduation had been in Kumasi. I could envision at least 20 family members in the audience. I thought about Bro. Kwabena.

Barely 2 months ago, we were discussing my future. I knew he would have been proud of me. He would have been happy that I was headed to college.

Through the tears, I spotted Pastor and Lamar. They were both waving at me with a huge smile. Bravely, I smiled back. Somebody had come for me. I did not have to go through graduation alone. Slowly, I pulled out my hand and gave them a quick wave. A third hand started to wave too. I was wondering who that was. Then I saw her bright lipstick! Bambi had come to my graduation. I smiled as I walked past them. I had worked so hard to get to this day.

Bowie High had a tradition of calling its graduates to the stage for their diplomas. As we lined up for the stage, I thought about how far I'd come. My journey from Kumasi to Accra. The move from Accra to New York. Enduring the harsh conditions at The Abbans'. Being basically 'rescued' by Bro Kwabena. And eventually ending up in Maryland. I thought about how fate had taken me to Ms. Mary's house and the friendship between me and her son. Despite the sadness buried deep down in me, I was optimistic about the future.

Then I heard my name over the loudspeaker. I smiled, stuck my chest out, and strutted across the stage. The cheers were loud. I couldn't believe it. I was a high school graduate.

After the ceremony, I walked up to my crew. Amidst smiles and tears, I listened to their congratulatory messages. Pastor offered to take us to Red Lobster. I was thrilled. Unfortunately, Bambi had another engagement and couldn't join us. It was okay. I was so happy that she had showed up for me.

I was impressed when I entered Red Lobster. The restaurant was beautiful and the warm biscuits were delicious. We had a great time. Lamar shared a lot of funny stories.

Thanks to Pastor and Lamar, my first time at a real restaurant was memorable. When I saw Pastor tip the waitress, I wondered how much I would make if I worked at Red Lobster. I couldn't see the work being any harder than what I was doing at McDonalds.

After dinner, Lamar offered to give me a ride home. I wondered about our future. Could we be more than friends? He gave me a hug when we arrived at the apartment. As much as I wanted to invite him into the apartment, I didn't. We said our goodbyes and I walked quietly up the stairs.

The next morning, as I sat around the sparse living room, I knew that It was time to start packing my bags. I could no longer afford to live in the apartment. It was in my best interest to find a place closer to my new school.

Luckily for me Lamar lived in Silver Springs which was not too far from school. He was going to help me find a roommate before the fall semester.

A

NEW CHAPTER

A NEW CHAPTER

On May 31, I moved from Bowie. Considering that I had found a temporary live-in job with the agency, I only needed a place to store my stuff.

My belongings fit into one suitcase and 2 cardboard boxes. Pastor offered to store the boxes at the church until I found a place. Since I needed my clothes, I held on to the suitcase.

Working the live-in job was great. I was able to make some money without thinking about rent and other bills. My only expense was for my meals. Paying for meals was manageable because a lot of the times, I ate my boss' leftovers.

The summer went by fast. When July rolled around I applied for the College Foundation scholarship to help alleviate the cost. Luckily, I was awarded $1,000 dollars towards my tuition. Combining that with the $500 initial scholarship translated into a tuition free education.

My next goal was to find a way to pay for my apartment, books and other expenses. This was when I decided to turn to credit cards to supplement my lifestyle.

Before long it was August and I still hadn't found a roommate. I had to act fast.

Against my better judgement, I decided to rent a room from Lamar until I could sort out my apartment situation. At that time, I did not anticipate any problems living with him. After all, we were good friends.

About a month into living with Lamar, our relationship began to change. We started spending more time together. Through our conversations, Lamar learned more about my 'paper' predicament.

The more we talked, the sorrier he felt for me. He realized that I was a cop away from removal.

One evening, Lamar came up with a grand plan. He was going to help me get a green card. He was going to marry me. The icing on the cake? He was not going to charge me a dime for our arranged marriage.

I was impressed. Most of the people who married for paper had to pay their spouses. I had heard of people charging as much as $10,000 for marriage paper. How good could my situation get?

By October, we were married. The ceremony was at the courthouse. We found 2 witnesses and boom, we had tied the knot. There was no fanfare. It was just a friend helping a friend out.

We had a plan. Lamar was going to file for me and then after I got my papers, we will get divorced. It all sounded great in theory.

However, it didn't quite work out the way I planned. Somewhere along the way, the lines became blurred and we started sleeping together. At first, it was all good.

Then I began to notice the late night calls and outings. Remember how Lamar had been a good listener and a friend to me? Well, he had the same relationship with at least 3 other girls. The only difference was that now I was his wife on paper.

How could I have fallen into this trap? I was competing with these girls for Lamar's attention. And because I came from a polygamous background, somehow I wasn't overly perturbed.

Although I was grateful that Lamar was willing to help me sort out my paper situation, our relationship wasn't what I had bargained for. Lamar was basically my first boyfriend turned husband.

Dealing with a cheating 'husband' was tricky. However, I was determined to stick with him because I needed my papers.

REVELATIONS

REVELATIONS

It was the Saturday before Christmas. I was listening to the newly elected President Clinton on TV when Lamar walked in. He told me that he had been laid off from work. I felt bad for him but then I thought that the situation was probably temporary.

3 months went by and Lamar hadn't gone back to work. Gradually he began acting like a desperate man. He would lose his temper at the least opportunity. If I voiced my opinion on an issue, Lamar will yell at me.

When the abuse started, I didn't even realize that I was a victim. First, it was the yelling, and then it graduated to full blown slaps.

I was terrified. I couldn't leave because I knew that I would have to show up at my immigration interview with him.

His bad attitude started permeating other aspects of his everyday life.

Sometime in April of 1993, Lamar got into a fight at a bar. He ended up destroying property and found himself in jail. When he was released, he came home with a black anklet. I didn't even know what it was. Apparently, he wasn't supposed to travel beyond a certain radius.

Well, he did not stick to the rules. By 8:00 pm that night, the police had him back in custody. I found out later that the device was an ankle bracelet designed for people who were either under house arrest or parole.

I visited Lamar in jail on a weekly basis. I needed to. Just in case I needed additional relationship evidence for my immigration interview.

Since he was waiting for trial, he was allowed to have visitors at least 3 times a week. However, due to my class and work schedule, I could only make it over the weekends.

Luckily for Lamar, he had a speedy trial. Before long, he was back home and back to his old habits. He drank himself to sleep and stopped looking for a job. In August we had to prepare for our interview. I was scared. What if something bad happened.

And happen it did. The day of our interview I had a morning class. Lamar told me that he will just meet me at the Immigration office. I prayed that he will show up. However, God did not hear my prayers that day.

I sat in the lobby for hours waiting for him. The man was a no show. I was terrified. What if my case was in jeopardy? What if Immigration denied my status?

Boldly, I walked up to reschedule our interview. I explained to them that my husband had not been feeling well and had hoped to show up. However, he was not well enough to be present. Luckily, I was able to reschedule the interview.

Now, I had a new problem. How in the world was I going to get Lamar to show up for our next interview? I had no idea.

On my way back home, I mulled over what I was going to say to him. I walked into the apartment and there he was. Sprawled out on the sofa. He hadn't even taken a shower all day.

My big mistake that day was asking Lamar why he didn't show up for the interview. Initially he did not respond so I kept pressing. This was my life. I was angry. I raised my voice at him.

Before I knew it, Lamar sprung out of that sofa. His fist came flying at my face. He beat me to a pulp.

When I woke up, I was lying on the floor with blood stains on the carpet. I dragged myself off the floor to the bathroom mirror. My face was swollen. Who was I going to report Lamar to?

I couldn't call the police. I didn't want trouble for myself.

A lightening bulb went off in my head. I knew that it was time to leave my abusive relationship.

Although I was in pain, I hurriedly packed my bag and left for Bambi's apartment. I had to escape. Who knew what Lamar was capable of?

COMING OF AGE

COMING OF AGE

I didn't have too many friends so it was easy for Lamar to figure out that I was staying at Bambi's. I guess when he sobered up he realized what he had done and wanted to make amends.

I was determined to stand my ground. There was no way that I was going back to our unhealthy relationship. Forget the paper situation. How much did I have to endure?

I don't regret leaving Lamar's that night.

I did not succumb to his efforts to try and win me back. The good news is that he agreed to go to the next immigration interview with me.

I was nervous when we arrived at the Immigration offices. Lamar and I no longer lived together. We were barely talking. What if the interviewer sensed our estrangement? I tried to smile. After all, we were supposed to be a couple. Luckily for me, my conditional status was approved. I was the new recipient of a temporary green card.

The card was temporary because Lamar and I had been married for less than 2 years. I would have to appear with him after our 2nd wedding anniversary to have the conditions removed. Meaning, I had to maintain some kind of relationship with him for a little longer.

Was I willing to give up my dignity for the sake of the paper? I thought long and hard before arriving at a decision.

I had 2 options. I could either stay with Lamar or walk away from our marriage. I took a leap of faith and chose the latter.

It was liberating! I had chosen to stand up for myself and my safety. I was not going to be lured back into an abusive relationship.

In my heart, I forgave Lamar. I was thankful for the opportunity to finally have legal papers. Although my paper was conditional, I was hopeful that I could navigate the rest of the immigration process.

In the next few months, I filed for a waiver to remove the condition on my green card. Maybe I was a step closer to the elusive American dream.

ONWARD!

ONWARD!

The night before the conditions were removed from my green card, I called the communication center in Kumasi. I needed Mama to get her prayer warriors together.

I needed that paper. It was my gateway to freedom. With 'papers', I will be able to apply for jobs that will pay better. I was worried about my mounting debt.

Because I was not earning enough money, I had resorted to using credit cards to supplement my everyday expenses. I had gotten to the point of using credit cards at the grocery store. I didn't have any reserves.

I reminded myself that I needed to stay positive. Graduation was close. I was about to receive my associate's degree.

With my papers in hand, I will be free to pursue my dreams! Maybe I could move into a safer neighborhood.

Chai, I will find a great job and make enough money to buy myself a car. And if it was God's will, I may be able to apply for a bachelor's degree program.

As I lay in the dark, I thought to myself. This Yankey life is full of ups and downs. Curveball after curveball.

MEET THE CHARACTERS

Sasha Yaa Asantewaa Badu– Protagonist

Ama Badu – Sasha's Mother

Kwame Badu – Sasha's Dad

Maame – Paternal Grandmother

Maa- Maternal Grandmother

Auntie Vivian – Midwife

Jahel – First Crush

Papa Gyan- Medicine Man

Bro Kwabena - Cousin

The Taylors – Accra Family

Awo – Maidservant at the Taylors

Mr. & Mrs. Abban – Diplomats (Related to Taylors)

Bambi – Bro. Kwabena's Girlfriend

Pastor – African Priest in America

Lamar – Sasha's Friend

Ms. Mary – Lamar's Mom

TIMELINE

Sasha is born

12 years old - She becomes a maidservant

13 years old – She moves to America

15 years old – She starts 8th grade

16 years old – She moves to Maryland

20 years old – Tragedy strikes

22 years old – The future awaits

The Human Oath

We are humans

Descendants of one species

Connected in ways we cannot comprehend

We are humans

We live by a creed

Together, we survive

We are humans

From all around the world

One kind only

And that is humankind

Marjy Marj

Glossary

A quick guide to the shimmigrant slang.

Aburokyire – Abroad

Aduane - Food

Akasanoma – Brand (Usually refers to TV or radio)

Alata Samina – Black Soap

Anigye – Happy

Asaase Yaa – Mother Earth

Atuu – Hug

Babylon – London

Bantama – Suburb of Kumasi

Bend Down Boutique – Consignment Clothing

Bofrot – Ghanaian Traditional Doughnut

Boneshaker – Local Bus

Boto – Black Powdery Substance / Herbs

Boys Quarters – Servants Living Quarters

Chai – Say What?

Chop Bar – Restaurant

Chow – Food

Compound House – Communal Living Abode

Dada - Dad

Don Dada – The Bigwig

Driver's Mate – Driver's Assistant

Glossary - Continued

Eh – Excuse me / What did you say?

Eish – What? / Oh Yeah?

Filla - News

Fofoofo - Cheap

Ghana Must Go Bag – Checkered Travel Bag

Kakra – Younger Twin

Kejetia – Name of a market in Kumasi

King Kong – Leader

Lorry fare – Bus or Taxi Fare

Ludu – Board Game

Mama - Mother

Me broni – My Special Person

Minerals - Soda

Mother mother – A Jumping Game

Nankonhwea – Skinny Legs

Nhyiaeso – Suburb of Kumasi

Nsekuo - Gossip

Obaa – Female

Obra- Life

Obroni – Caucasian

Obroni wawu – Consignment Apparel

O'level – Ordinary Level Exam (British exam)

Oo – I see/ Got it

Oto – Yam / Plantain Birthday Meal

Glossary - Continued

Onyame - God

Oware – Pebble Game

Paper (s) – Legal Documents (Green Card)

Panyin – Older Twin

Piesie – First Born

Saito – Public School

Santaase – Suburb of Kumasi

Self-Contained House – A house built for one family

Shank – Brand of Toilet / Poop

Shito – Black Pepper

Tolee – Lies / Jokes

Tomantoes - Tomatoes

Top Dawg – Top Friend / Person

Trotro - Bus

Tweaa – Say What?

Twedeampon Nyame – Omnipotent God

Wahala - Trouble

Walayi – This is hard

Yaa – Born on Thursday

Yankey - America

To all the immigrants of this earth-

Be not dismayed

CPSIA information can be obtained
at www.ICGtesting.com
Printed in the USA
LVHW032359210520
656258LV00004B/1205